For Tien and Reid
—M. A.

BEACH LANE BOOKS

An imprint of Simon & Schuster Children's Publishing Division
1230 Avenue of the Americas, New York, New York 10020
Text copyright © 2017 by Cynthia Rylant
Illustrations copyright © 2017 by Mike Austin
For information about special discounts for bulk purchases, please contact
Simon & Schuster Special Sales at 1-866-506-1949 or business@simonandschuster.com.
The Simon & Schuster Speakers Bureau can bring authors to your live event.
For more information or to book an event, contact the Simon & Schuster Speakers Bureau
at 1-866-248-3049 or visit our website at www.simonspeakers.com.
Book design by Lauren Rille
The text for this book was set in Bauer Bodoni.
The illustrations for this book were rendered in Adobe Illustrator and Adobe Photoshop.
Manufactured in China
0717 SCP
10 9 8 7 6 5 4 3 2
CIP data for this book is available from the Library of Congress.
ISBN 978-1-4814-4523-8
ISBN 978-1-4814-4524-5 (eBook)

written by
CYNTHIA RYLANT

illustrated by
MIKE AUSTIN

Henny, Penny, Lenny, Denny, and Mike

Beach Lane Books
New York   London   Toronto   Sydney   New Delhi

Henny, Penny, Lenny, Denny, and Mike
are five fish who met at the fish store.

They are fab friends.

A little girl brought them home
and plopped them into the tank:

PLOP
PLOP PLOP
PLOP
PLOP

The fish tank
is like HEAVEN.

Penny loves
the diver.

Henny loves the
orange gravel.

Lenny loves
the rock.

FiSH OOD

Denny loves
the pirate ship.

And Mike loves
the bubbles.

Nobody loves
the snail,
but that's okay.

This is fish-tank life:

Swim SWIM Swim

Henny, Penny, Lenny, Denny, and Mike think that being a fish is

So FAB!

They smack kisses to the little girl every day.

There is only one day when fish-tank life is not so fab.

It is . . .

They are UNCEREMONIOUSLY plopped
into a BOWL.

Then the little girl makes
the orange gravel,
the diver,
the pirate ship,
the rock,
and the whole big fish tank
JUST SPARKLE.

WOW!

Everything is so CRISP!
The diver is impeccable.
The ship is ship-shape.

(But, alas, the snail
is still ignored.)

Can fish-tank life be any
more perfect than this?

Why, YES!

Because . . .

PLOP!

Well hello, CLOWNFISH!

The clownfish is such
a clown. He starts
telling joke after joke
and Henny, Penny,
Lenny, Denny, and
Mike laugh so hard, their
bubbles fizz up the whole tank.

But wait.
There's more. . . .

TADA!

PLOP!

An ANGELFISH!

Henny, Penny, Lenny, Denny, and Mike stop yukking it up and they . . . just . . . stare.

She is so BEAUTIFUL.

But wait.
There's more. . . .

GLUNK!

It's . . . a . . . FAIRY CASTLE!!!

Henny, Penny, Lenny, Denny, and Mike forget
all about clowns and angels.

They are all about the FAIRY CASTLE.

It is enchanting.
It is ornamental.
It is exotic.
It is . . .

A TRAP!

Help! Lenny is stuck!

Oh no! say Henny, Penny, Denny, and Mike.
What to do?

The clownfish tries to lighten the mood with a joke.
The angelfish begins to pray.
Yet nothing unsticks Lenny.

But wait . . .

It is a snail!
A snail on a mission.

The quick-thinking snail (who everyone had ignored)
slides right up to Lenny, and with one fell SUCK . . .

Lenny is unstuck! The tank explodes into cheers.

Henny, Penny, Lenny, Denny, and Mike
smack kisses all over the snail.

The clownfish yuks it up.

The angelfish sings hallelujah.

And fish-tank life returns
to what it always was . . .

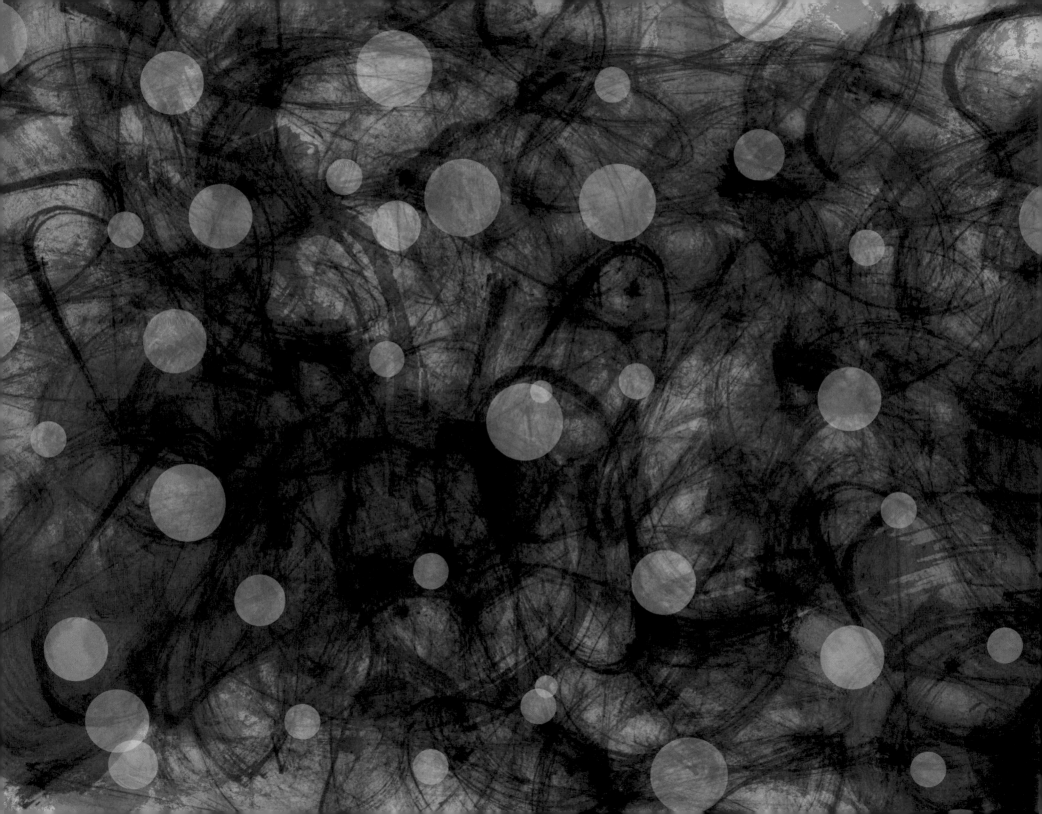